How to Draw
HARRY POTTER FOR KIDS

EASY & FUN

STEP BY STEP DRAWINGS

1

2

3

4

5

6

HARRY POTTER

PRACTICE PAGE

HERMIONE
GRANGER

PRACTICE PAGE

RON
WEASLEY

PRACTICE PAGE

PROFESSOR
DUMBLEDORE

PRACTICE PAGE

SEVERUS
SNAPE

PRACTICE PAGE

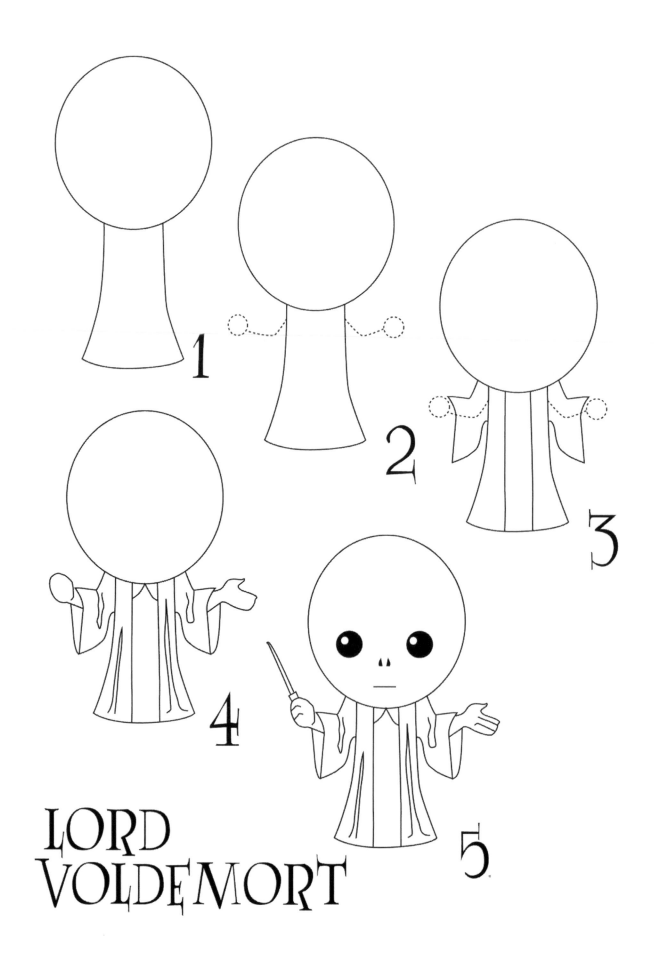

LORD
VOLDEMORT

PRACTICE PAGE

DOBBY

1

2

3

4

5

6

PRACTICE PAGE

1

2

3

4

5

6

HAGRID

PRACTICE PAGE

1

2

3

4

5

6

PROFESSOR
MCGONAGALL

PRACTICE PAGE

1

2

3

4

5

6

LUNA
LOVEGOOD

PRACTICE PAGE

ALASTOR
"MAD-EYE"
MOODY

PRACTICE PAGE

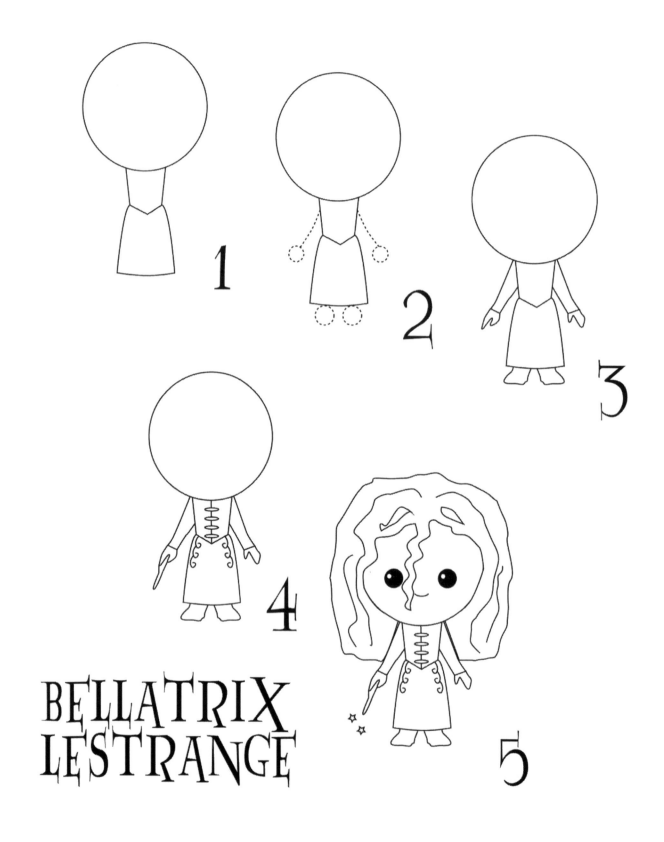

1

2

3

BELLATRIX
LESTRANGE

4

5

PRACTICE PAGE

1

2

3

4

NYMPHADORA TONKS

5

PRACTICE PAGE

1

2

3

4

5

QUIRINUS
QUIRRELL

PRACTICE PAGE

1 2 3 4 5 6

GINNY
WEASLEY

PRACTICE PAGE

GEORGE
WEASLEY

PRACTICE PAGE

1

2

3

4

5

MOANING
MYRTLE

PRACTICE PAGE

1

2

3

4

5

DOLORES
UMBRIDGE

PRACTICE PAGE

1

2

3

4

5

DRACO
MALFOY

PRACTICE PAGE

SIRIUS
BLACK

1

2

3

4

5

6

PRACTICE PAGE

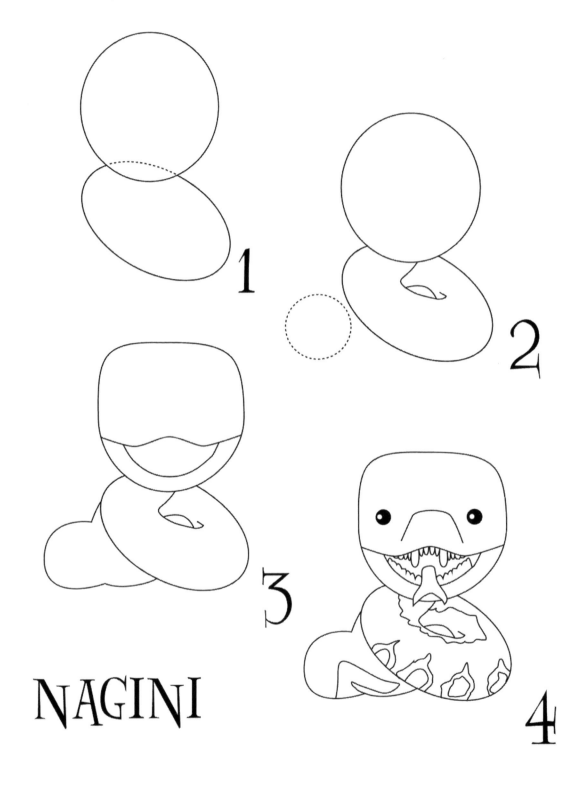

NAGINI

PRACTICE PAGE

1

2

3

4

5

REMUS
LUPIN

6

PRACTICE PAGE

NEVILLE
LONGBOTTOM

PRACTICE PAGE

1

2

3

4

5

6

NEARLY
HEADLESS
NICK

PRACTICE PAGE

FLEUR
DELACOUR

PRACTICE PAGE

PROFESSOR
TRELAWNEY

PRACTICE PAGE

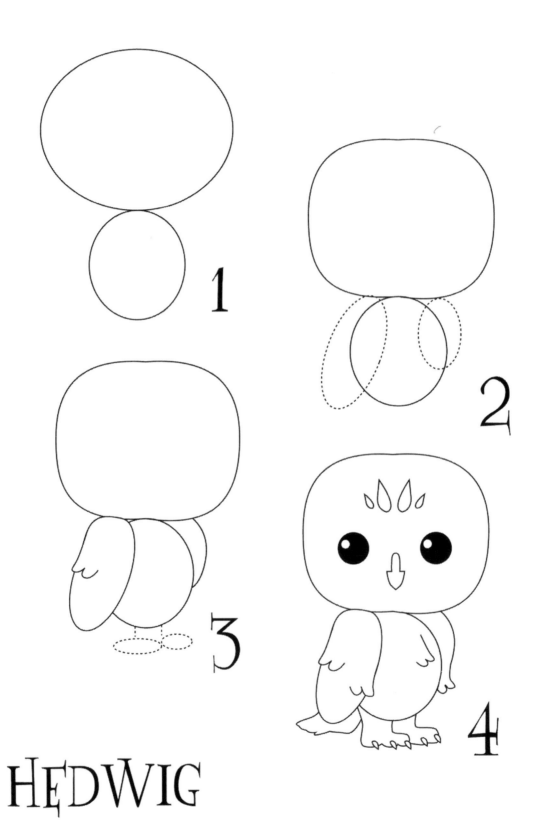

1

2

3

4

HEDWIG

PRACTICE PAGE

Printed in Great
Britain
by Amazon